附錄 A

Single-camera film format
單鏡拍攝格式

Sample Script Pages
劇本範例頁

PERFECT PITCH

FADE IN:

EXT. VAN NUYS APARTMENT - MORNING

A 12-year-old tagger, not unlike a pit bull, leaves
his mark on a fire hydrant outside this dreary stucco
complex.

It's a picture-perfect day in the Valley. Not a cloud
in the beige sky.

An ALARM CLOCK GOES OFF.

INT. STUDIO APARTMENT

A feminine arm shoots out of the covers and gropes a
bedside table for the ALARM. Knocks a pair of glasses
onto the floor. Keeps searching. Tips an empty coffee
mug onto its side. Finally finds the clock and hits
snooze. The ALARM GOES SILENT.

The arm drops back onto the bed.

The ALARM CLOCK TICKS.

VENETIAN BLINDS

RATTLE almost imperceptibly.

OVERTURNED COFFEE MUG

rocks gently back and forth.

WIDE ON APARTMENT

Silence for the longest time. Then all hell breaks
loose.

The ROOM SHAKES VIOLENTLY. The bed hops like a spastic
rabbit. Pictures drop off the walls.

The COFFEE MUG falls and SHATTERS.

ASPIRING SCREENWRITER

explodes from beneath the covers, eyes wide with terror
as her APARTMENT QUAKES around her. GRETCHEN PFLUM.

Beside her bed a computer monitor sways violently, tips and topples.

Gretchen dives. Gets tangled in the sheets. Hits the floor just as the MONITOR SMASHES over the top of the printer.

And then it ALL STOPS. Just like that. Gretchen looks around the apartment. It's an unbelievable mess. So's she. Early 20s, she's rumpled and badly shaken. But so darn cute you don't care.

Seven seconds of silence. And then the PIPES over her head BURST. WATER DRENCHES the apartment.

EXT. GRETCHEN'S APARTMENT - MORNING

The door is flung open. Gretchen staggers outside. Rumpled, shaken and now soaked. But still cute. CAR ALARMS are BLARING. DOGS are BARKING. Neighbors are spilling from their apartments. Gretchen looks around, spots an elderly woman in a muumuu.

                    GRETCHEN
          Stella, what just happened? What
          was that?!

STELLA toddles toward Gretchen, utterly unruffled.

                    STELLA
          Oh, I'd say about a six point one
          or six point two. Have a muffin,
          dear.
                    (hands Gretchen one
                    and glances at her
                    watch)
          Didn't you have a meeting this
          morning?

Gretchen blanches.

                    GRETCHEN
          Oh no.

INT. GRETCHEN'S APARTMENT

She appears in the doorway. WATER continues to RAIN DOWN.

                    GRETCHEN
          Oh no.

She plunges into the room.

Steps over fallen items to her computer. Sees the
shattered monitor atop the printer.

                    GRETCHEN
          OH NO.
                    (a cry from the
                     depths)
          MY PITCH!!!!!!!!!!

She starts to dig. Heaves the monitor to the floor. Her
PHONE RINGS. She looks for it. Can't find it. It KEEPS
RINGING. In frustration she kicks the monitor shell.
Unearthing the phone. She answers.

                    GRETCHEN
          Hello?

                    GRETCHEN'S MAMA (V.O.)
          Baby?

INTERCUT WITH:

EXT. KANSAS FARM - ENDLESS WHEAT FIELD - DAY

GRETCHEN'S MAMA in the air-conditioned, glassed-in
cockpit of a massive, modern combine, mowing down wheat.
She's got a cell phone to her ear. A RADIO PLAYS LOW in
the b.g.

                    GRETCHEN
          Mama?

                    GRETCHEN'S MAMA
          Listen, baby, I can't talk long
          but I want you to Fed Ex me some
          more of that good mango salsa.

Gretchen picks gingerly through the broken glass that
litters her computer equipment. She pulls a stack of
soggy pages from the printer.

                    GRETCHEN'S MAMA
          Your father and I drizzled it over
          our grilled salmon last night
          and --

                    GRETCHEN
                    (starting to cry)
          Mama, I just had an earthquake.

                    GRETCHEN'S MAMA
          An earthquake? Are you sure,
          baby?

                         GRETCHEN
                      (crying harder)
              Of course I'm sure --

                         GRETCHEN'S MAMA
              Because I've got on C.N.N. and
              they're not saying a thing about
              an earthquake.

Gretchen looks at the destruction all around her.
Doesn't know what to say.

                         GRETCHEN
              Mama, I've got to go. I have a
              very important meeting and I
              overslept and then the earthquake
              woke me up --

                         GRETCHEN'S MAMA
              Well there you go! Blessing in
              disguise.
                      (then)
              Gotta go, baby. Don't forget the
              salsa. Kisses.

She clicks off. Leaving Gretchen remembering why she
fled Kansas in the first place.

                                        CUT TO:

EXT. APARTMENT BUILDING - PARKING LOT - GRETCHEN'S CAR -
DAY

A WHIMPERING sound as Gretchen rushes up, dressed, her
hair still wet. She hears the sound and looks around.
Sees nothing. Unlocks her door. The WHIMPERING again.
She looks beneath her car.

HER POV UNDER CAR

A dirty, frightened CHIHUAHUA cowers, CRYING.

                         GRETCHEN (O.S.)
              Hey there, Taco Bell, what's
              wrong?

BACK TO SCENE

Gretchen extends her arms. The dog races from under her
car and leaps into them. She laughs.

                    GRETCHEN
          Earthquake scare you, little guy?
                    (beat)
          Listen, I've got to run. Where do
          you belong?

The little dog licks her face.

EXT. STUDIO GATE - DAY

Gretchen pulls up to the guard shack in her '83 Civic. A
GUARD steps up to the car.

                    GUARD
          Going to see?

                    GRETCHEN
                (intimidated)
          Ian von Blitzenkrantz.

                    GUARD
          The producer?
                (looks over her sad
                 little car)
          Here to dust his Oscars?

Something rises up inside Gretchen. She is, after all, a
screenwriter.

                    GRETCHEN
          No, I'm not here to dust his Oscars.
          I'm here to win him another one.

The Guard is duly impressed by her moxy.

                    GUARD
          Name?

                    GRETCHEN
          Gretchen Pflum. P-F-L-U-M.

The Guard checks his list.

                    GUARD
          Don't see it.
                (looks inside car)
          And you can't bring in the dog.

The little chihuahua sits on the passenger seat. Eating
Gretchen's pitch.

                    GRETCHEN
          No, no, no!!!

She pulls the half-eaten pages from the dog's mouth.
They're beyond salvage.

                    GRETCHEN
      Oh noooooooooo!!!

INT. PRODUCER'S OFFICES - RECEPTION AREA - DAY

A hard-driving young executive WANNA-BE jabbers into a
telephone headset while he surfs the Web. Everything he
says he says fast.

                    WANNA-BE
      Von Blitzenkrantz Entertainment...
      He'sinameetingcanwereturn?

He looks up as Gretchen enters.

                    WANNA-BE
        (to phone)
      Holdplease.
        (to Gretchen)
      Helpyou?

                    GRETCHEN
      Gretchen Pflum. I have a meeting
      with Mr. von Blitzenkrantz. I
      may be a little, um... late.

                    WANNA-BE
      HaveaseatI'lllethimknowyou'rehere.
      Wantanythingtodrink?
      Coffeesodawater?

Gretchen takes a beat to decode his spiel.

                    GRETCHEN
      Oh. Well. Um. Water.

She smiles.

                    WANNA-BE
      Bottled or tap?

                    GRETCHEN
      Oh. Um. Bottled.

                    WANNA-BE
      Perrier or Evian?

                    GRETCHEN
      ... Perrier.

                              WANNA-BE
                Room temperature or refrigerated?

Gretchen just stares.

                                        DISSOLVE TO:

INT. RECEPTION AREA - LATER

Time has passed. Lots of time. The bottle of Perrier is
empty. Gretchen's trying to piece together what's left
of her tattered pitch. The Wanna-Be is still on the
phone.

                              WANNA-BE
                NoIhaven'treadthescriptI'vereadthe
                coverage. Greatcoverage. Huge
                coverage. BestcoverageI'veever
                read. PluginOrlandoorMattorWill
                andyou'vegotahit.

                                        DISSOLVE TO:

INT. RECEPTION AREA - LATER

The Wanna-Be is gone. Gretchen still waits. Finally, a
voice like a foghorn bellows from O.S.

                              VOICE (O.S.)
                Jason?!... Jason?!... Jason?!...
                Jason?!

A puffy-faced guy in his 50s pads out in his bare feet.
IAN VON BLITZENKRANTZ. He sees there's no one behind the
desk. Spots Gretchen.

                              VON BLITZENKRANTZ
                Who are you?

                              GRETCHEN
                Gretchen Pflum. I'm supposed to
                pitch to Mr. von Blitzenkrantz.

He stares at her an uncomfortably long moment. At long,
long last:

                              VON BLITZENKRANTZ
                Okey-dokey.

INT. VON BLITZENKRANTZ'S OFFICE - DAY

Movie posters from his Oscar-winning films cover the
walls. Statuettes litter the desk. Gretchen sits on the
couch, dry-mouthed and tongue-tied, leafing through the
pages of her prepared pitch. Von Blitzenkrantz waits.

                    VON BLITZENKRANTZ
          So, sweetheart. Now's when you
          tell me a story.

Gretchen looks up like a deer caught in the headlights.
Clears her throat. Sets the pages aside. And begins.

                    GRETCHEN
          A studio apartment in Van Nuys.
          An alarm clock is ringing.
          There's a girl --

                    VON BLITZENKRANTZ
          How old?

                    GRETCHEN
          Early twenties.

                    VON BLITZENKRANTZ
          Good. We'll get that chick from
          "Alias."

                    GRETCHEN
          The girl's in bed. She's
          overslept.

                    VON BLITZENKRANTZ
          Who's she with?

                    GRETCHEN
          Who's she with? Um... she's
          alone.

                    VON BLITZENKRANTZ
          She's alone?
                    (guffaws)
          How interesting is that?!
                    (then)
          No, seriously.

                    GRETCHEN
          Well... okay... she's not
          completely alone. There's a dog.

                    VON BLITZENKRANTZ
          What kind of dog?

                         GRETCHEN
          Chihuahua.

                    VON BLITZENKRANTZ
          Chihuahuas are hot right now. I
          like the way you think.

                         GRETCHEN
          Then this massive earthquake hits.
          BANG!!!

          She slams her hand down on the coffee table. Von
          Blitzenkrantz nearly jumps out of his skin. He cocks his
          head and studies Gretchen. At long last throws his hands
          straight up in the air and exclaims:

                    VON BLITZENKRANTZ
          I love this stuff!!!
                    (stands)
          I gotta pee.
                    (heads for the door)
          But you keep going. You're doing
          great.

          He disappears. Gretchen looks around the empty office.
          Shrugs. And keeps going.

                         GRETCHEN
          So the bed starts jumping around
          like a spastic rabbit, the girl is
          like insane with fear --

          Gretchen gets up and crosses to the enormous desk.
          Admires the Oscars there.

                         GRETCHEN
          But she doesn't care, she's got
          the first pitch meeting of her
          life and nothing is going to stop
          her.

          She spots a little dust on one of the statuettes. Buffs
          it with her sleeve.

                         GRETCHEN
          But then she sees her computer
          monitor about to crash onto her
          only copy of her perfect,
          wonderful pitch. She dives! And
          snatches that bad boy out of the
          air!!!

Gretchen smiles like the sunrise. 'Cause she's in
Hollywood now.

FADE OUT.

THE END

《完美提案》

淡入：

EXT. 凡奈斯區某公寓 ── 早晨

一名十二歲的塗鴉者，跟比特犬沒什麼兩樣地，在陰鬱沉悶的灰泥公寓外一個消防栓上留下了他的記號。

這裡是聖弗南多山谷，今天的天氣好得不能再好了。萬里無雲，天空一片湛藍。

突然間鬧鐘鈴聲大作。

INT. 公寓的套房

一隻纖纖素手很快地伸出被子外，在一邊的床頭櫃上四處摸索著鬧鐘。她不小心把眼鏡推落到地上後，仍然沒有停下來，接著又打翻了一個空的馬克杯。最後，她終於找到鬧鐘，並且按下了貪睡鍵，鬧鐘的鈴聲嘎然而止。

手臂的主人將手縮回到床上。

鬧鐘繼續發出規律的滴答聲。

百葉窗的葉簾

以幾乎無法察覺的方式發出嗒嗒聲。

翻倒的馬克杯

輕輕地來回晃動。

公寓的遠景

經過了長時間的靜默，突然之間天下大亂。

房間劇烈地搖晃著。床鋪晃動得像是隻抽搐不止的兔子。牆上掛著的畫都掉了下來。

馬克杯摔破在地上，碎片四濺。

野心勃勃的劇作家

從被窩裡彈了出來，張大的雙眼裡充斥著恐懼，因為整間公寓都在搖晃。她是格雷琴·芙蘭。

在她床邊的一台電腦螢幕正隨著震動而劇烈搖晃著，一番掙扎後終於倒下。

格雷琴想衝下床，但是身體被散亂的被單給纏住了。當她摔到地上的時候，電腦螢幕正好整個砸碎在印表機上。

突然間，一切都停止了，就這樣。格雷琴環顧房間四周，一片慘不忍睹。不只是她的公寓滿是混亂，她自己也是一團糟。她大約二十歲出頭，這場突來的災難使她看起來驚慌失措而且邋遢不堪，但是你一點都不會在意，因為她長得實在是太迷人了。

安靜了七秒鐘之後，她頭頂上方的水管爆裂開來，水淋濕了整個公寓。

EXT. 格雷琴的公寓 ─ 早上

公寓的門被猛然地打開，格雷琴跟跟蹌蹌地走到戶外。她衣著凌亂、全身發抖，而且從頭到腳都濕透了，但這一點都沒有影響到她的可愛樣貌。汽車防盜器的警鈴此起彼落響著，附近的狗都在狂吠，鄰居們也都陸陸續續衝出他們的公寓。格雷琴環伺著周遭的一切，然後目光停留在一位身穿夏威夷連衣裙的老婦人。

> 格雷琴
> 史黛拉，到底發生什麼事了？剛剛那是什麼？

史黛拉不急不徐地走向格雷琴，十足泰然自若的神氣。

> 史黛拉
> 喔，我想大概是 6.1 或是 6.2 級左右的地震吧。來個瑪
> 芬蛋糕如何？親愛的。
> 　　（遞給格雷琴一個瑪芬蛋糕後，瞄了眼她的手錶）
> 妳今天早上不是要開會嗎？

格雷琴臉刷地一下變白。

> 格雷琴
> 噢！不。

INT. 格雷琴的公寓

她出現在門口。自天花板上噴出的水持續傾洩而下。

> 格雷琴
> 噢！不。

她衝進房間裡。

她踩在四處散落的物品上，走向她的電腦。她驚慌地看著印表機上碎裂的電腦螢幕。

> 格雷琴
>
> 噢！不！
> （放聲大哭）
> 我的提案！！！！！！！！！

她開始到處翻找。她將螢幕抬起來放到地上。然後，她的手機突然響了。她四處搜尋，卻怎麼都找不到手機。同時間鈴聲持續響著。一氣之下她踢了螢幕外殼一腳，卻因此歪打正著地發現了手機。她接起電話。

> 格雷琴
>
> 哈囉？

> 格雷琴的媽媽（V.O.）
>
> 寶貝？

切換至：

EXT. 坎薩斯的農場 ─ 一望無際的麥田 ─ 白天

格雷琴的媽媽正在一台巨大的現代聯合收割機的玻璃駕駛艙內，開著冷氣收割小麥。她把手機移到耳邊。廣播小聲地在背景播放著。

> 格雷琴
>
> 媽？

> 格雷琴的媽媽
>
> 聽好，寶貝，我不能講太久，但我要妳再快遞給我上次
> 那些好吃的芒果莎莎醬。

格雷琴小心翼翼地將散落在電腦設備四周的碎玻璃撿起來。她從印表機裡抽出一疊濕透了的紙張。

> 格雷琴的媽媽
>
> 妳爸和我昨晚把一些莎莎醬灑在烤鮭魚上，然後──

> 格雷琴
>
> （開始哭了起來）
> 媽，剛剛地震了。

> 格雷琴的媽媽
>
> 地震？妳確定嗎，寶貝？

格雷琴
（哭得更大聲了）
當然確定啊——

格雷琴的媽媽
我才剛聽過CNN新聞，他們沒有報導任何和地震有關的
消息。

格雷琴無力地看著四周亂七八糟的一切，無言以對。

格雷琴
媽，我得掛電話了。我要去開一個非常重要的會，但是
我睡過頭了，然後被地震搖醒——

格雷琴的媽媽
妳看！賽翁失馬焉知非福！
（接著）
我要掛電話了寶貝。別忘了寄莎莎醬給我。親親。

她喀嚓一聲地掛了電話。這讓格雷琴回想起為什麼她當初要從堪薩斯逃出來。

切換至：

EXT. 公寓 — 停車場 — 格雷琴的車 — 白天

梳洗打扮後的格雷琴頂著一頭濕漉漉的頭髮跑向她的車子，不知從哪裡傳來一陣嗚咽
聲。她聽見這奇特的聲響後四下張望，卻什麼都沒有看到。當她解開車鎖後，嗚咽聲
又出現了。她往車底下看去。

車底下，她的主觀鏡頭
一隻髒兮兮又飽受驚嚇的吉娃娃，怯生生地縮成一團悲鳴著。

格雷琴（O.S.）
嘿，小塔可餅，你怎麼了？

回到場景

格雷琴伸出雙臂。狗從車底下衝出來，跳到她的懷中。她笑出聲來。

格雷琴

被地震嚇到了對吧，小可愛？
（停頓）
聽著，我在趕時間。你家在哪裡呢？

小狗逕自舔著她的臉。

EXT. 片廠大門 — 白天

格雷琴把她的1983年本田civic停在警衛室旁。一名警衛走向她的車。

警衛

要找誰？

格雷琴

（膽肮的）
伊恩・馮・布利茲卡蘭茲。

警衛

那個製作人？
（打量著那台辛酸的小破車）
來這幫他的奧斯卡獎盃撢灰塵嗎？

格雷琴內心升起了一股無名火。說到底，她也是一名劇作家。

格雷琴

不，我不是來幫他清理奧斯卡獎盃的。我是為了替他贏
得另一座奧斯卡獎而來的。

警衛很欣賞她大無畏的回答。

警衛

名字？

格雷琴

格雷琴・芙蘭。芙——蘭。

警衛低頭查看訪客名單。

警衛

我在預約名單上沒看到妳。
（往車裡看）
而且妳也不可以帶狗進去。

小小的吉娃娃坐在副駕駛座上，正啃著格雷琴的劇本提案。

格雷琴

不、不、不！！！

當她從小狗的嘴裡抽出被啃到只剩半截的稿子時，一切都太遲了。

　　　　　　　　　　格雷琴
　　　　天————哪！！！

INT. 製作人的辦公室 — 接待處 — 白天

一個活力充沛、夢想有一天要成為大人物的年輕接待員，正一邊逛著網頁，一邊對著電話耳機急促而含混不清地說著。他講話的速度快得讓人發暈。

　　　　　　　　　　大人物夢想者
　　　　這裡是馮・布利茲卡蘭茲演藝事業……
　　　　他正在開會我們稍後回電好嗎？

他抬頭看向正走進來的格雷琴。

　　　　　　　　　　大人物夢想者
　　　　　　（對著電話）
　　　　請稍等。
　　　　　　（對著格雷琴）
　　　　有什麼事嗎？

　　　　　　　　　　格雷琴
　　　　我是格雷琴・芙蘭。我和馮・布利茲卡蘭茲先生有約。
　　　　我有點……呃……遲到了。

　　　　　　　　　　大人物夢想者
　　　　先坐一下我會跟他說你來了。
　　　　妳要喝點什麼嗎咖啡汽水還是水？

格雷琴停頓了一下，試圖解開這如謎般嘰哩咕嚕的一句話。

　　　　　　　　　　格雷琴
　　　　喔。好。嗯。水就好。

她對著他微笑。

　　　　　　　　　　大人物夢想者
　　　　瓶裝水還是自來水？

　　　　　　　　　　格雷琴
　　　　喔。嗯。瓶裝水。

　　　　　　　　　　大人物夢想者
　　　　沛綠雅還是依雲牌的？

　　　　　　　　　　格雷琴
　　　　……沛綠雅。

大人物夢想者

常溫還是冰的？

格雷琴只是睜大了眼睛。

溶接至：

INT. 接待處 — 稍晚

經過了一段時間。其實是很長一段時間。沛綠雅的瓶子裡已經一滴水都不剩。格雷琴試著拼湊支離破碎的提案殘骸。接待員仍然在講電話。

大人物夢想者

沒有我還沒有讀過劇本但我看了劇本的分析報告。很棒
的報告讓人印象深刻的報告真的是我讀過最棒的分析報
告了。把奧蘭多或麥特或是威爾加入劇本裡保證會爆紅。

溶接至：

INT. 接待處 — 稍晚

接待員不知所蹤，而格雷琴還在等。終於，一個像霧警喇吧般的怒吼聲自畫面外傳來。

聲音（O.S.）

傑森！……傑森？！……傑森？！……
傑森？！

一個臉頰臃腫、約五十多歲的男子赤著腳啪嗒啪嗒地從裡面走出來。他就是伊恩‧馮‧布利茲卡蘭茲。他看到辦公桌後面沒有人，接著他看到了格雷琴。

馮‧布利茲卡蘭茲

妳是哪位？

格雷琴

格雷琴‧芙蘭。我有劇本提案要給馮‧布利茲卡蘭茲先
生。

他盯著她看了好一下子，時間久得讓人感到渾身不自在。最後終於再度開口：

馮‧布利茲卡蘭茲

好吧。

INT. 馮・布利茲卡蘭茲的辦公室 — 白天

牆上掛滿了他贏得奧斯卡獎的那些電影海報。書桌上到處都是小金人獎盃。格雷琴坐在沙發上，除了緊張到口乾舌燥之外，舌頭也像打結了似地說不出話來。她翻著她所準備的劇本提案，馮・布利茲卡蘭茲等著她開口。

馮・布利茲卡蘭茲

那麼甜心，現在告訴我妳有什麼好故事吧。

格雷琴看起來像隻在黑夜裡被汽車大燈照射而僵住的鹿。她清了清喉嚨，把稿子放到一旁，然後開口了。

格雷琴

在凡奈斯的某個公寓套房裡，鬧鐘的鈴聲不停地響。有個女孩——

馮・布利茲卡蘭茲

多大？

格雷琴

二十出頭。

馮・布利茲卡蘭茲

很好！我們可以找《雙面女間諜》裡的那個小妞來演。

格雷琴

這個女孩在床上。她睡過頭了。

馮・布利茲卡蘭茲

她和誰在一起？

格雷琴

她和誰在一起？ 嗯……她單獨一個人。

馮・布利茲卡蘭茲

她單獨一人？
　　（一陣狂笑）
那實在太好笑了！
　　（然後）
不可能吧，說真的？

格雷琴

嗯……好吧……她不完全是一個人。還有一隻狗。

馮・布利茲卡蘭茲

哪個品種的狗？

> 格雷琴

吉娃娃。

> 馮‧布利茲卡蘭茲

吉娃娃是現在當紅的寵物。我很欣賞妳的思考方式。

> 格雷琴

接著一個強烈的地震來襲。砰！！！

她說話的同時，手掌也重重地拍了咖啡桌一下。馮‧布利茲卡蘭茲被這突如其來的舉動嚇了一跳。他把頭歪向一邊，端詳著格雷琴。過了好一陣子後，他把兩手往空中一伸並且大喊：

> 馮‧布利茲卡蘭茲

我愛死這個故事了！！！
　　（站起身來）
我得上個小號。
　　（走向門）
別停下來。妳做得很好。

他消失於門後。格雷琴環顧這個除了她之外空無一人的辦公室，她聳聳肩，然後繼續她的故事。

> 格雷琴

然後床開始像隻抽搐的兔子般跳動，女孩因為恐懼而開
始歇斯底里——

格雷琴站了起來，走向那張大辦公桌。靜靜地欣賞放在桌上的奧斯卡獎盃。

> 格雷琴

但是當她冷靜下來後，她變得不在意了，因為她即將前
往生平第一次的提案會議，沒有任何事可以阻擋她。

她看到眾多獎盃裡的其中一個上面有點灰塵。她舉起衣袖拭去灰塵，露出原本光亮的金屬色澤。

> 格雷琴

但是當她看到她的電腦螢幕即將掉落並毀了她僅存的那
個完美、絕妙的提案紙稿時，她衝上前去，在半空中一
把攔截住那個螢幕！！！

格雷琴笑得如旭日初昇般的燦爛。因為她終於夢想成真地踏進好萊塢了。

淡出。

<u>全劇終</u>

附錄 B

Multi-camera film format
多鏡頭拍攝格式

Sample Script Pages
劇本範例頁

BETTER FRED THAN DEAD

"A Simple Sample"

ACT ONE

(A)

FADE IN:

INT. "BETTER FRED THAN DEAD" DINER - DAY
(Fred, Martha, Debbie, Bob, Curt, Diner Extras)

IT'S THE BREAKFAST RUSH. FRED'S BEHIND THE COUNTER.
MARTHA'S TAKING AN ORDER FROM DEBBIE, EARLY 20S,
ATHLETIC, LEAN.

                    DEBBIE

          Ham and cheese omelet, side of

          bacon, coffee.

                    MARTHA

          (KNOWING) Atkins diet.

                    DEBBIE

          Yes, ma'am.

                    MARTHA

          (CALLS TO FRED) Ham and cheese

          omelet, bacon.

                    FRED

          Comin' atcha.

HE CLIMBS ONTO THE DINER COUNTER.

                    (MORE)

                    FRED (CONT'D)

Yo. Yo yo. Your attention right

here, if you please. As you may

know, we're all appearing in a

half-hour multi-camera television

production.

                    MARTHA

(LOOKING PAST CAMERA) That would

explain the live audience in the

bleachers, Fred.

                    FRED

Yes it does.

THE FRONT DOOR OPENS. BOB ENTERS.

                    FRED (CONT'D)

What it doesn't explain is the

deplorable lack of humorous

dialogue, pratfalls and the like.

BOB SLIPS ON A BANANA PEEL AND HITS THE DECK IN A
MASTERFULLY EXECUTED BIT OF PHYSICAL COMEDY.

                    FRED (CONT'D)

I stand corrected.

                    MARTHA

So anyway --

                    FRED

So anyway, what we have here is a

little piece of situation comedy.

A simple little sample, as it

were. But lacking a certain

je ne sais quoi.

                    MARTHA

There, you've said it. What we

have here --

                    FRED

Is a situation.

                    MARTHA

Without the comedy.

CURT COMES THROUGH THE FRONT DOOR AND SLIPS ON THE BANANA
PEEL. HE TAKES OUT AN ENTIRE ROW OF TABLES ON HIS WAY DOWN.
IT'S A SIGHT TO BEHOLD.

SFX: THE O.S. AUDIENCE LAUGHS.

                    DEBBIE

I stand corrected.

SFX: THE PHONE RINGS.

NO ONE ANSWERS IT. CURT LOOKS UP FROM WHERE HE LIES ON
THE FLOOR.

                    CURT

Anyone gong to help me up?

                    DEBBIE

Nope.

                    FRED

Not a chance.

                    MARTHA

Don't look at me. The longer

you're on the floor, the funnier

it gets.

SFX: THE AUDIENCE HOWLS.

CURT CLIMBS TO HIS FEET. FRED CLAPS HIS HANDS FOR
ATTENTION.

                    FRED

          Eyes this way, people. (WAITS)

          So that's about it. (TURNS TO

          O.S. AUDIENCE) How'd we do?

SFX: HUGE APPLAUSE.

EVERYONE IN THE DINER STANDS, FACES THE AUDIENCE AND
BOWS.

                              DISSOLVE TO:

《好傢伙弗瑞德》

〈一個簡單的實例〉

<u>第一幕</u>

(A)

淡入：

INT.「好傢伙弗瑞德」快餐店 — 白天

（弗瑞德、瑪莎、戴比、鮑伯、柯爾特、餐館的背景演員）

這是早餐的尖峰時段。弗瑞德站在吧檯後方，瑪莎正在為戴比點餐。戴比大概二十歲出頭，有著運動員的體魄，相當精瘦。

　　　　　　　　戴比

　　我要一份火腿和起司歐姆蛋，另外單點培根和咖啡。

　　　　　　　　瑪莎

　　（示意她懂）低醣飲食法。

　　　　　　　　戴比

　　是的，女士。

　　　　　　　　瑪莎

　　（呼喊弗瑞德）火腿和起司歐姆蛋，還有培根。

　　　　　　　　弗瑞德

　　馬上就來。

他爬到餐館的吧檯上。

　　　　　　　（更多）

弗瑞德（續）

喂、喂、喂。拜託大家，注意一下我這裡好嗎？你們可能已經知道了，現在我們所有人都在這個半小時長的多鏡頭電視節目裡面。

瑪莎

（看著攝影機後方）這說明了為什麼高腳座位上有現場觀眾坐著，弗瑞德。

弗瑞德

沒錯。

前門打開了。<u>鮑伯走進來</u>。

弗瑞德（續）

但是並沒有解釋為什麼沒有幽默的台詞、令人發笑的滑倒動作等等之類的東西。實在有夠可悲的。

鮑伯踩到香蕉皮而摔倒在地上，完成一場精彩的動作喜劇。

弗瑞德（續）

我錯了。

瑪莎

所以——

弗瑞德

所以不管怎樣，我們這裡上演了一齣小小的情境喜劇。如剛才所發生的，一個簡單的實例。但就是少了點⋯⋯我也不知道是什麼。

瑪莎

你說得沒錯。我們這裡看到的是——

弗瑞德

是情境。

瑪莎

但沒有喜劇。

柯爾特從前門進來，然後踩到香蕉皮而滑了個四腳朝天。他摔倒的同時，也連帶撞倒了整排的桌子。那景象還真令人嘆為觀止。

SFX：畫面外的觀眾哄堂大笑。

戴比

我錯了。

SFX：電話響了。

沒人接聽。柯爾特從他躺著的地板往上望著遙不可及的電話。

柯爾特

沒有人要扶我起來嗎？

戴比

沒有。

弗瑞德

想都別想。

瑪莎

不要看我。你待在地上越久，你就越搞笑。

SFX：觀眾縱聲大笑。

柯爾特從地板上站起身來。弗瑞德拍著雙手以取得大家的注意力。

弗瑞德

請大家看一下這邊。（等待）我們演完啦！（轉向畫面外的觀眾）我們表現得怎麼樣？

SFX：熱烈掌聲。

餐館裡的所有人都站了起來，面向觀眾並且彎腰鞠躬。

溶接至：

附錄 C

Title, Cast and Sets Pages
標題、演員卡司、場景頁

Sample Script Pages
劇本範例頁

這是簡易的待售劇本標題頁，只有一位作者，而且沒有特殊題材來源。你需要寫上的
資訊就只有這些。

PERFECT PITCH

written by

Gretchen Pflum

12902 Hollywood Place
Burbank, CA 91505
(818) 555-9807

《完美提案》

著作

格雷芩·芙蘭

12902 好萊塢
柏本克，加州 91505
(818) 555-9807

這是電視影集裡單集的標題頁，這個劇本由兩個作家共同創作完成。不論是一個小時或是半小時長的電視劇本，它們的標題頁看起來都是一樣的。

BETTER FRED THAN DEAD

"A Simple Sample"

written by

John Gretel & Isaac Mott

JOSHUA McMANUS PRODUCTIONS
Bungalow 15
10202 W. Washington Boulevard
Culver City, CA 90232

REV. FIRST DRAFT

August 2, 2008

《好傢伙弗瑞德》

〈一個簡單的實例〉

著作

約翰格特爾 & 艾薩克摩特

喬許・麥可邁努斯 製作公司
15棟
10202 西華盛頓大道
柯芙市,加州 90232

修訂版本 初稿

2008年8月2日

Rev. 07/13/08 (Blue)
Rev. 07/15/08 (Pink)
Rev. 07/16/08 (Yellow)
Rev. 07/21/08 (Green)

這是正在製作中的院線電影劇本標題頁，其中包含了所有參與撰寫的作家名字、稿件類別和日期，以及修訂日期與紙張顏色的列表（包含現行使用版本的資訊）。

12 HOURS IN BERLIN

written by

Felix Alvin Butler Jr.

revisions by

Maria Gustav
Charles Knowles-Hilldebrand
Robert Bush

current revisions by

Johan Potemkin

FINAL DRAFT

July 12, 2008
© 2008
MICHAEL GELD PRODS.
All Rights Reserved

MICHAEL GELD PRODUCTIONS
4000 Warner Boulevard
Burbank, CA 91505

修訂版 07/13/08（藍色）
修訂版 07/15/08（粉紅色）
修訂版 07/16/08（黃色）
修訂版 07/21/08（綠色）

《柏林十二小時》

著作

小費利斯 · 愛爾溫 · 巴特勒

修訂

瑪莉亞 · 格斯塔夫
查爾斯 · 諾維斯—希爾德布蘭德
羅伯特 · 布希

最新修訂

約翰 · 波特金

完稿

2008 年 7 月 12 日
© 2008
麥克格爾德製片公司
版權所有

麥可格爾德製片公司
4000 華納大道
柏班克，加州 91505

NINE LIVES

"Cats Away"

CAST

KITTY

JULIO MENDEZ

HILDE SCHMIDT

FELIX SIMPSON

LIEUTENANT MARTIN

MAX

REBECCA BEAKER

GUARD #1

GUARD #2

DR. SRINIVASAN

LYLE

SAM

TODD

MRS. BRACKMAN

ROTO-ROOTER GUY

這是一小時長的電視影集單集的卡司列表。有台詞的角色依出場順序來做排列。另外，一種常見的排列方式是將固定出現的角色放前面，其餘的角色則依出場順序放後面，背景角色則不用編入名單內。卡司頁不要編頁碼，此外，待售劇本不要加卡司頁。

《九命嬌娃》

〈貓去無蹤〉

演員陣容

凱蒂

朱利歐・曼德茲

希爾德・史密特

費利斯・辛普森

馬丁中尉

麥克斯

雷貝卡・畢克

警衛 #1

警衛 #2

史理尼范森醫生

萊爾

山姆

陶德

布拉克曼太太

水管工人

NINE LIVES

"Cats Away"

CAST

KITTY...MARSHA WILLIAMS

JULIO MENDEZ...............................ALEX GONZALEZ

HILDE SCHMIDT..........................ALISON PARMENTER

FELIX SIMPSON....................MICHAEL PAUL MILLIKAN

LIEUTENANT MARTIN.......................ANTHONY BOGNA

GUEST CAST

MAX...TIM FISH

REBECCA BEAKER.............................SYLVIA SIMMS

GUARD #1..................................N. KELLY LYON

GUARD #2..................................JAMES BEISE

PARKING LOT EXTRAS
POLICE HEADQUARTERS EXTRAS

半小時長的電視影集單集演員列表方式如上。劇中角色的名字列在左側，演員的名字列在右側。正規的演員通常都是按照固定順序排列，而客串演員則依照出場順序排列。背景演員以出場順序依序放在客串演員下面。卡司頁不要編頁碼。此外，待售劇本不要加卡司頁。

"Cats Away"

SETS

INTERIORS:

KENNEDY HIGH SCHOOL
  Main Office
  Science Lab
  Library
  Girls' Bathroom

NEW YORK STOCK EXCHANGE

STORM SEWERS

POLICE HEADQUARTERS
  Holding Cell
  Detectives' Bullpen

McDONALD'S RESTAURANT

STAPLES CENTER
  Escalator
  Luxury Suite
  Basketball Court
  Visitors' Locker Room

FUNERAL HOME

EXTERIORS:

PARK

SCHOOL PLAYGROUND

NEW YORK STOCK EXCHANGE

DUMP
  Front Gate

SOUTH L.A. STREETS

POLICE HEADQUARTERS

McDONALD'S RESTAURANT

STAPLES CENTER

CEMETERY

VENICE BEACH

這是一小時長電視劇的場景列表。主要場景是依照出現順序來排列,次要場景則是歸類在主要場景底下。場景頁不需要頁碼。此外,待售劇本不要放場景頁。

《九命嬌娃》

〈貓去無蹤〉

場景

室內場景：

甘迺迪高級中學
　主要辦公室
　科學實驗室
　圖書館
　女廁

紐約證券交易所

地下道

警察總局
　拘留所
　警探的辦公室

麥當勞餐廳

史泰博體育場
　手扶梯
　豪華包廂
　籃球場
　訪客置物櫃

殯儀館

室外場景：

公園

學校的操場

紐約證券交易所

垃圾場
　前門

南洛杉磯街道

警察總部

麥當勞餐廳

史泰博體育場

公墓

威尼斯海灘

NINE LIVES

"Cats Away"

SETS

Teaser, Scene A - Int. Detectives' Bullpen - Day

Act One, Scene B - Int. Kitty's Apartment - Kitchen - Night

Act One, Scene C - Int. Kitty's Apartment - Bedroom - Night

Act One, Scene D - Int. Detectives' Bullpen - Morning

Act Two, Scene E - Int. Empire State Building - Elevator -
                   Later That Day

Act Two, Scene F - Int. Detectives' Bullpen - Same Time

Act Two, Scene G - Int. Empire State Building - Lobby -
                   30 Minutes Later

Tag, Scene H - Int. Kitty's Apartment - Night

這是半小時長的電視影集場景列表的範例。這些場景列表頁可能以很多不同形式來表示，但是幾乎每個場景數字或是場景字母都是依場景出現順序而編排的，並且編排的和對應它們的場景一起列出來，即便同樣的場景不斷重複出現。場景頁不需要頁碼，此外，待售劇本不要加入場景頁。

《九命嬌娃》

〈貓去無蹤〉

場景

預告，場景A — Int. 警探的辦公室 — 白天

第一幕，場景B — Int. 凱蒂的公寓 — 廚房 — 夜晚

第一幕，場景C — Int. 凱蒂的公寓 — 臥室 — 夜晚

第一幕，場景D — Int. 警探的辦公室 — 早上

第二幕，場景E — Int. 帝國大廈 — 電梯 — 當天稍晚

第二幕，場景F — Int. 警探的辦公室 — 同一時間

第二幕，場景G — Int. 帝國大廈 — 大廳 — 三十分鐘過後

最後一幕，場景H — Int. 凱蒂的公寓 — 夜晚

NOTE

NOTE

NOTE